To Daniel,
S.McB.

For Steve,
A.J.

First published 2007 by Walker Books Ltd
87 Vauxhall Walk, London SE11 5HJ

10 9 8 7 6 5 4 3 2 1

Text © 2007 Sam McBratney
Illustrations © 2007 Anita Jeram

Guess How Much I Love You™ is a registered
trademark of Walker Books Ltd, London

The right of Sam McBratney and Anita Jeram to be
identified as author and illustrator respectively of this
work has been asserted by them in accordance with
the Copyright, Designs and Patents Act 1988

This book has been typeset in Cochin

Printed and bound in China

British Library Cataloguing in
Publication Data: a catalogue record
for this book is available from the
British Library

ISBN 978-1-4063-0856-3

www.walkerbooks.co.uk

# GUESS HOW MUCH
# I LOVE YOU

*in the*

# WINTER

Written by

## Sam M<sup>c</sup>Bratney

Illustrated by

## Anita Jeram

WALKER BOOKS
AND SUBSIDIARIES
LONDON · BOSTON · SYDNEY · AUCKLAND

Little Nutbrown Hare
and Big Nutbrown Hare went
out in the winter snow.

They played I Spy as they
hopped through the snow.
Little Nutbrown Hare
looked around until he
saw something interesting.

"I spy something that belongs
to a tree," he said.

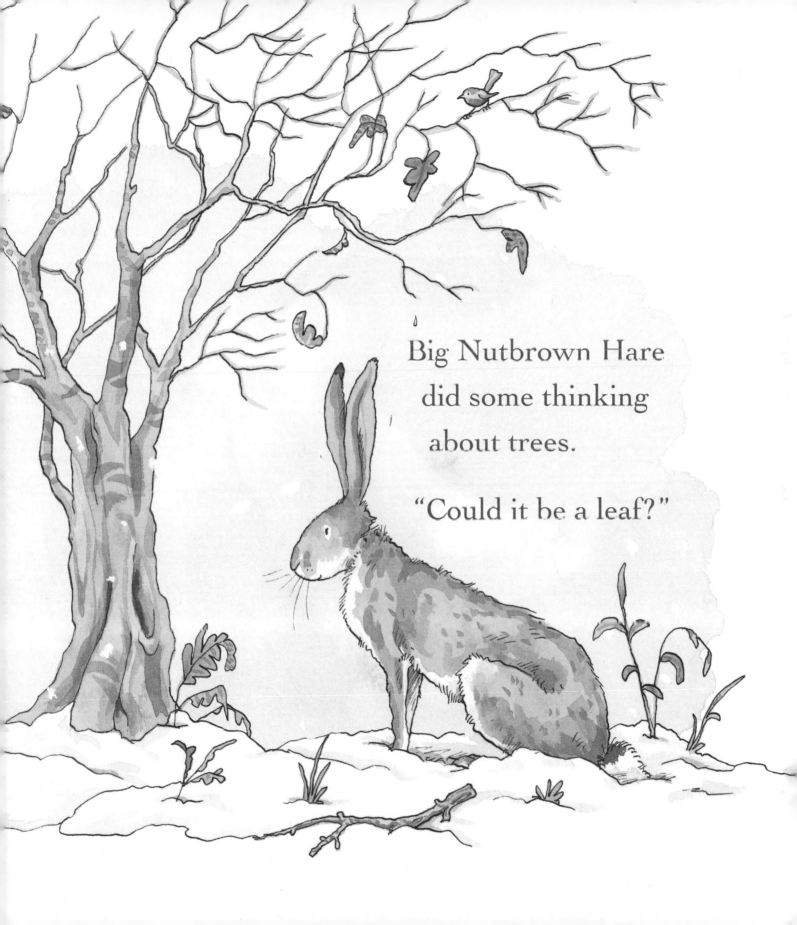

Big Nutbrown Hare
did some thinking
about trees.

"Could it be a leaf?"

It was the right answer!

Now it was Big Nutbrown
Hare's turn to look around him.

"I spy something that
belongs to a spider."

"A web!" said
Little Nutbrown Hare.

Yes! A web was the answer.

"I spy something that
belongs to a bird," said
Little Nutbrown
Hare.

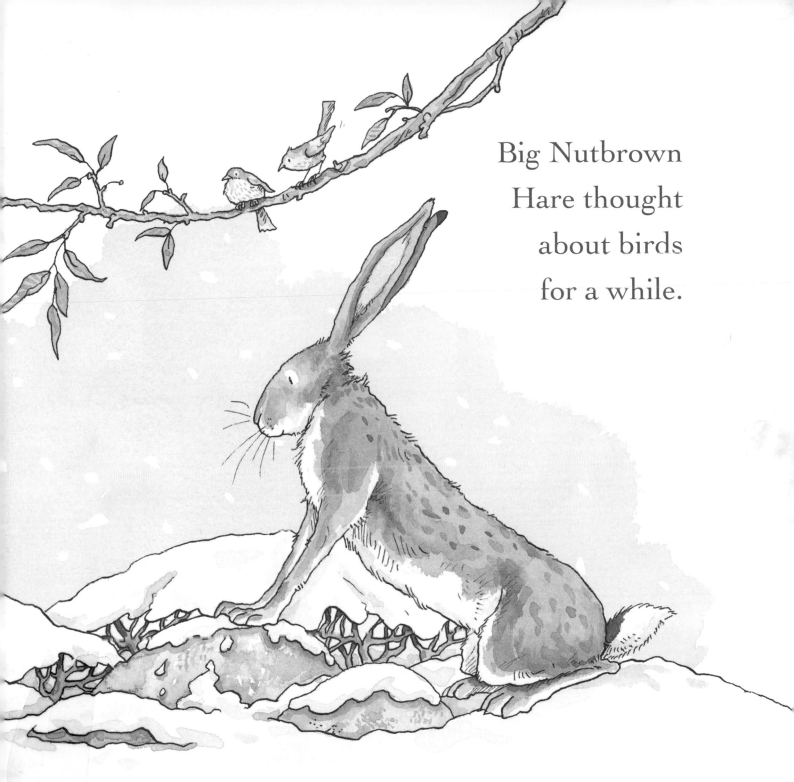

Big Nutbrown Hare thought about birds for a while.

Then he said, "Could it be a feather?"

Yes! It was a feather.

"This time," said
Big Nutbrown Hare, "I spy something that
belongs to the river. And it's wet, wet, wet."

"Water!" cried Little Nutbrown Hare.

Water was the answer.

Little Nutbrown Hare began to laugh.
I've got a good one, he thought.
"I spy something that belongs to me."

Big Nutbrown Hare was puzzled.
"Can I have a clue?" he said.

"It's only there when the
sun comes out."

"Your shadow!" said
Big Nutbrown
Hare.

Then Big Nutbrown Hare said,

"I spy something that belongs to *me*
and it's not my shadow."

This was a really tricky one.
Little Nutbrown Hare did some
thinking, and then he said,

"Can I have a clue?"

"It's little... It's nutbrown...
It's my most favourite thing...

And it can hop."

"Me!"